2DAYS LOVE

TODAYS LOVE THAT IS MOSTLY TWO-DAYS LOVE

JOSHIT MISHRA UDITANSHU

""*Every thing in life has an end. But never all the things and opportunities can end together.*"

~ Joshit Mishra 'Udianshu' ."

Just read and think about it!

Poem destiny on last page.

Contents

Preface

Oh yeah! Finally I've omitted myself to writing. Basically today is 22nd of March 2021 and tomorrow is my last internal assessment that is ASL of English and after that , guess! I will be free for almost a week. Not enough? No! But I would this time try something new. So I've decided to write a short story about a relationship or more accurately a teenage relationship. It might get longer but let's start anyway. Here a character who is going to be the narrator himself is my friend . During last lockdown we had long and long phone conversations and meanwhile he hinted me an interesting story of his friend circle and at the same time asked me not to disclose it . And you see I'm here. Okay but it's necessary because it's the story of almost every teenager nowadays. That friend of mine is Siddharth . Siddharth or shortly Sid, a charming guy of 16 is in eleventh class. A height of 5'8" makes him look better than ever. He has a girlfriend that is one of his classmates and her good name is Avantika or shortly Avni . Basically both have a good understanding of one another but at the same time they are quarrelsome. Navi ~ a childhood friend of Avni , has just got introduced with Sid by the means of there tution classes. They have two coaching classes with a time gap of 30 minutes in betweet 'em. Adam ~ a friend of Sid is too in the same batch of both coachings. Actually the story is going to flourish around these four characters mainly. That day I was at school doing nothing . It was one of those post-lockdown physical class. After returning from school, I found that my tutions were suspended for the day. Out of peaks of boredom,I made a phone call to Sid , and he told the story in much more depth and details.He had given only hints earlier. In subsequent days I were in touch with Sid and he explained everything. Whatever he narrated is ahead.→

Joshit Mishra 'Uditanshu' 21 March 2022

Prologue

The counting had reached one and a half hundred. I opened and saw a group having some random name of its. I opened and basically the chatting there seemed to be second part of some discussion already done elsewhere. It mainly contained phrases like "It is a great trouble." "I might get restricted in home." "Mine future is too now destroyed." "Now nothing can be done!" " I'm feeling like crying." "There's no solution." " Maybe we are finished now!" " What will they think about us!" "Have we broken there trust?" " Why these problems for us?" " We haven't done a mere wrong deed!". I patiently read all those messages and now I doubted if everything was alright. As I reached the latest texts I saw there my name being repeated.. "Sid!" "Sid listen no!" "Here we are in big trouble..."~and some twenty texts of similar meaning in a line.

CHAPTER ONE

THE DISCUSSION

"Thinking is the first step towards creating something whereas curiosity full of determination is the most important brick of foundation."
~ Joshit Mishra Uditanshu

[1]

"Don't you think Sid?" Avni texted "Navi is having some crush on Adam."

"NO" I replied "What makes you think so?"

She replied- "Nothing,but won't it become a better thing to get those childish youngsters together?"

"I don't think you should intrupt this natural procedure of developing crush on and further making decisions to Carry on or not.."

"I was just thinking about it.."

"Wouldn't it had been better if you had shown such a thoughtfulness in our matter,I think we would have been in a better relationship with much greater mutual trust"

"Oh!stop talking rubbish, I have full trust on you,but ain't sure about yours ..!"

"Don't try to divert me , you took a quite long time to propose me"

"Was it my solemn responsibility to propose, couldn't have you taken the initiative?"

"Don't be fool , you could have done it earlier,I was cautious about our boards" said Sid with intelligence. "Anyway , focus upon present"said Avni.

"See again you are trying to divert me...."

And went the conversation endlessly unless either of them was called up by their respective parents lol! I would like to draw your attention towards the fact that it is the first hypothetical origin of the relationship of our concern .

[2]

Our four characters and a girl(,let's name her Q) are standing outside there first tution classes. Sid and Avni are standing at one metre separation from the rest and hence divided in two groups. Let's leave whatever those three were discussing and focus upon me that is narrator and simply Sid

Avni said-"Sid!"

I replied "Yes please!"

"Sid...!!" ~ spoken with her extreme cuteness.

"Speak no!"

"Don't you think they are having mutual crush on one another?"

"What do you think?"

"I'm damn sure , they must have!"

"I'm going to support your views though I don't find any point in it..!"

"You ain't the last honest person on this earth, I see"~said Avni with heavy sarcasm and a gesture full of loveful anger.

"I totally agree with you , my babe..!"~ said I with a sarcasm full of crafty gesture and extreme politeness.

“That’s better now!”and now the smile,the best experience of the day!,oh! Let’s leave that all and focus upon our matter as she is having many things that need a detailed explanation for my Shake.

“As you please.”

“Okay! Leave that all, tell me, do you have any clue if they know...?”

And came the previous batch of students out! Already Avni was hating her juniors and now she is going to hate them more than ever. I was getting bore this day , but I always hated this moment. Q gave a gentle nudge to me and said “how is it Sid? Getting some more closer ha! Keep it up boss” and proceeded further teasing me. To sum up , Avni again took on imaginary matter before me that I found no point of relevance within. By the way she kept a mum about it for a quite long period of time ~2 hour.LoL!

[3]

The same day Avni again approached me during the walk between two tutions ..... Those three were walking few metres ahead and I was behind beside Avni . She again raised the matter of Navi! Means was that this much important that she is with me and ignoring this she was busy in some other matter! Okay this thing made me somewhat more serious towards her this conversation. This contradicts the fact that every conversation with gf is only useless nuisance which should be kept in mind only upto she is before me. I was just saying ok ok. Then she started quoting many things that she felt were the initial signs. I just thought those two immature teens with one another,the thought was terrible as like placing sodium pallets in water.

[4]

The very next day , Avni again met me outside first tution. Let me clear a thing, these all consequences are happening during the first week of the December. Now Avni was more cheerful today. She again raised the matter of Navi in front of me. Oh no! I wanted to talk over random matters by staring at her face and she now seems a little wacky. But her keen interest over this matter now raises an internal pressure to do some help of her. Okay , now I was confessed to tell her the observations of mine. Buy meanwhile she intrupted! Won't she let me think over this matter? She said -

"Sid you try to know what's inside Adam's mind and I'll try the same on Navi"

I got amazed-"What! How can I just ask this rubbish?"

"Because I'm asking you to do!"

"No, I won't."

"Don't you want to go back to your home on your own feet?"~ said Avni with a gesture full of anger but overflooded by love and cuteness. Now I became speechless. Though I knew that it isn't going to be in real but I for the sake of her confessed . Avni happily proceeded ~

"Okay then you proceed to observe Adam and I do Navi."

"As you wish!"

"And one thing more , don't ask directly unless you are confirm about it ..."

And went the conversation so on unless juniors batch came out.

[5]

"Do you remember Avni When we first became friends?" ~ texted Sid.

"I think I forgot to keep it as a special record"

"What! You must remember these! Okay when did you propose me?"

"Sorry no! I don't have any idea! I must have forgotten.."

"What you don't have any interest over ours...."

And hence we started quarrelling over no matter and finally ended up with break up. LoL! Then following two days we didn't speak even a word to one another, once or twice ours eyes met and that said eager to patch up but neither Iniciated and hence a year long relationship of ours ended up forever..and the twilight that we together saw of linkage between Navi and Adam was broken and they were now seperated into poles apart. Hence the relationship of Avni and me was over and so was of Adam and Navi~that wasn't even flourishing! This is how a weak bond breaks.. This is the case of most of teenage relationships. The fight/ quarrel over other's matters and then end up breaking up and hence destroying the fruitful thoughts of people around them.

[6]

Tell me one thing, when you don't see a special teacher in your school for last few days , don't you become curious to know where he/she is busy? The same manner should have proceeded in the matter of Avni and me.. What! You had guessed it .. Such a thoughtful and intelligent readers I have ! Okay, let's return to the context. As mentioned earlier Avni and I broke up. Q, Adam, and Navi noticed it but said almost nothing in first day. On second day first of all Q started something like scolding me in absence of Avni but I rarely replied to her and simply listened to her with utmost patience..Then the same day , we returned from second tution and it was ten minutes earlier than usual. We walked towards the stadium, when we were outside the side gate of stadium, Adam asked me why I had such a repulsive behaviour towards Avni . That area didn't had any kind of lightning.. the only thing that made us stop there without getting afraid of darkness was tha light that was coming out from the well kindled stadium. The gloomy surrounding and cold breez of early December made me feel my nose freezing. To be precise there were three people~ Adam , I and another friend of ours who need not get mentioned here. The only sound that could intrupt us was from the cheers of goals or wickets.. I asked from that friend of ours a little space of privacy. He started riding bicycle in a circular manner at some distance from us. There was about 100 sq. feet area empty where we were standing. Then we started our conversations. He said ~

"From where have you got to know all about it?"

"It was clearly visible from the behaviour of you two that there is surely something unusual."... I kept a mum and my expressions showed a stron dissatisfaction. He continued after a pause during which he analysed my dissatisfaction.."Avni told me all that happened between you two."

"No I don't think there any matter between us , infact I don't see anything between us now , everything is over now."

"Don't be such a foolish, there is such a well established and perfectly working relationship of you two but you are trying to spoil it all over such a nonsense matter."

"Don't take her side okay! And the thing you are referring to as non sense means a lot for atleast me."

"Oh see yourself that she and even such dates related to her means a lot for you even after this quarrel and you are trying to convince me for everything over."

"I thought she would Iniciate today but her behaviour showed no sign of apology."

"But she is hurt too."

''I don't think so."

"You said her something go to hell and those words had worked there part of destruction well."

"Oh means she has disclosed everything!"

"May be!"

"So you expect that I'm going to apologise and sort all this."

"Yup!"

"So I'm not going to do any such activity because she has the major part of mistakes this time."

"Okay I'll discuss with her."

"That's better."

Then a stillness for a few moments. That boy was still bicycling in the same circular manner. I broke the silence ~

"You have some crush over navi no."

"Are you mad?"

"Your gesture speaks a lot about it."

"No there's nothing like that!"

"You have!"

"No!"

"Yes you have."

"No I don't."

"Not a little bit."

"No!"

"Neither a further smaller one?"

"No!"

"But I think you #ave!"

"No I don't have."

"Oh. But your actions speak well about it all."

"I am damn sure that there's nothing like that."

"May be but the glitter in your eyes and sparkle in your gesture has another impact."

"There's nothing like that"~ this time he turned away from me a bit. Now I was sure that Avni was right over this Matter and he surely has crush over Navi... We than moved near to that friend and then had some random talks...

[7]

The same evening at about 9 I texted navi. "Is she there?"

"Yes, she is."

"Should I approach?"

"Yes you should. She seems disappointed a lot." I took the step forward and texted Avni with a confusing emoji~ "Hii "

Quickly came the reply as if she was just waiting for me to text "Hlw."

"I'm sorry for all that happened."

"Yeah! Atleast you realised the truth that not always I'm wrong!"

"I was expecting an apology from your side."

"Thought came to my mind to accept the guilt that I haven't even done ; and I was about to message you only after five minutes."~ this just stroke at my heart. These words made me feel even worse. I just felt like I'm the one wo forces her .... By the way to duck the serious discussions and a more dipressive out come I replied~

"Oh shit! Just missed by five minutes."

"Ain't you getting to behave yourself? Means seeking profits in everything even if those profit doesn't worth a bit."

Then Avni again raised the matter of Adam and I told her whatever has happened at stadium site . I was just bored of this , so I just wanted to throw this subject out of our conversation at any cost. But today too only Adam was widespread over our conversation as she wasn't accepting the fact that Adam don't have any such feelings and I was trying to confess her just one time so that she won't raise this all again. I thought I had done my part of job and would be free nowon but she always kept them amidst our discussion and I just kept placing it in direction she wanted . Well you shouldn't make your veiw that I was totally satisfied with the answers of Adam as I'm that kind of guy who keeps on investigating till I get satisfactory results. At the same time I don't let my mind work even for a second if I don't see any profit. Second habit overcame the first one.

CHAPTER TWO

THE DILEMMA

“"Observations can be easily affected by external factors. Always use your intellectual logics before believing your eyes."”

~Joshit Mishra 'Uditanshu

[1]

Basically this phase arose due to a picnic trip to a nearby place with our teacher (tution teacher) And somewhat matters from two tutions. First of all we should focus upon trip. During this period even I started getting confused for what the truth was .. Let me clear, there are only two people with this mental complications; no third person even was indulged in it . Sir announced the trip a week before and our excitement was at some other level. But there was one person who was busy solving the problem of complex relationship ~ my Avni bro! From where should we pick it up?.. let's take it from a day before.. Nope! Let's only take the day of picnic trip. We were given the time of 5:30 AM to report at the tution centre. I set three alarms but woke up before any of them rang! Prepared for trip rechecked my bag, pack took a look of mine , put mobile in pocket and sat behind daddy on bike and headed towards tutions.....

[2]

As I reached tution centre , the first boy I saw was~ guess ~ Adam! He was wearing a jacket over t shirt and a jeans. There were a few more standing outside covering the gate . I walked inside the tution classes but lo! It was preoccupied by crowd of girls gathered there! There was place left where rarely all boys could have put there bag packs but we did . I took a quick glance, all were there but where the heck Avni was? At the same moment she entered from backside door , dressed in long suit (probably that's what it is called , I'm not sure) of blue colour (it was dark blue perhaps I'm not sure this time too) with vertical strips on it . She sat on some first bench and as I moved outside, found Adam standing at door looking inside. I followed his eyesight, it was navi ! Seriously! Was she ? I tried to confirm it but he had changed his focus this time and was gazing at me as prepared to nudge me as I too was staring at Avni . Okay this must have only a hallucination. I should confess . Meanwhile he nudged and said "continue to stare at your crush, Today the whole day is yours....".I just smiled keeping in mind " dude you have stated working over it far before me."

[3]

We then sat in bus , went to first stoppage looking at the beauty of forest and gazing at the deers antelopes and many more. There is nothing special during this journey of our interest apart from views that I captured in my soul . When we stopped to have some tea, as I'm not kind of person who loves tea was sitting in bus with Adam and a few more. Adam played a proper country song and cracked laughter ~ this perhaps disturbed Navi who was sitting at back side of bus and then she started scolding Adam . We pawed our way out. Adam asked Navi to pass out the bag !

Isn't it surprising that she got moulded within minutes and passed it. Anyway after two minutes we descended the bus and moved a little further, at our return we again found her along with Avni , Q and another girl complaining for we missed the chance of a photoshoot. It didn't mattered for me but It seems had a better after effect for adam! During the next half of journey we kept playing country , bhojpuri and folk songs and our sir was too enjoying it. But they kept shouting over it and no one was there to pay attention to them except one , because of whom we stopped such nuisance~ guess who~ obviously our Adam! LoL!

[4]

Let me clear a thing, Navi and Adam are friends themselves, they have had friendly quarrels, she used to say him "Rakksas" meaning devil and he always slap her on her cheeks which has a solid reason that I'll tell you later. Navi for nothing kept hitting Adam friendly or lovingly to be precise.. Now let's return to our picnic trip, we were playing volleyball and Navi wasn't. She came several times in between our match and hit Adam the same way and ran away adjusting her specks. Amazingly Adam just gave a glittering smile to her actions that were never expected! Then we played damsharash where both showed there competitive spirits. This way there intense tussle continued.

[5]

Now comes the turn of most important moments of our picnic trip~for Adam and Navi okay!, Not for me because I already had my part apart which I'll discuss in my story. Basically I was sitting facing the river and behind me Adam and navi were standing facing one another and there line of sight was perpendicular to mine. Now Navi teased Adam by lipsing the name of his seventh standard crush. Adam made a movement as if he was to beat Navi~that wasn't a percent true~but navi trying to escape put two or three steps backwards got bruised her leg a bit. Adam didn't notice it at that time and went back to his gang. Now Navi sat at a little distance from me but I was lost in beauty of nature and didn't even noticed what had happened. Avni noticed the wound and first comforted Navi and then aggressively approached Adam. Now he got a lot tensed! Searched for first aid kit but didn't get anything. Still he used all of his mind and took~guess what?~ turmeric powder from cooking staff and quickly reached near Navi. Exactly at this point I came out of myself and noticed all the hue and cry. Explaining to this latter, Navi said ~

"It was for the first time in my whole life that after being injured I was feeling the best!"

I asked~ "Then did he applied turmeric powder on the wound himself?"

"Don't be foolish! It's not any movie scene. It's my life!"

"Then?" Then he gave it on my hand and stood as a visitor."

"Oh!"

Then she stayed at the same place for a quite long duration and Adam kept wondering here and there with Navi as center. Feeling thirsty! Navi tried to stand up and fetch water bottle from her bag but as a scene of romantic movie, Adam stopped her from doing so and himself fetched for her. Again water bottle had no trace of water on it ,then Adam asked a boy standing nearby who took water bottle, filled it from water cane and then handed it over to Adam. Adam gave it to Navi, she drank it and again it was Adam who jogged to put it back in bag. Again while returning, our instructor asked us to take utensils and other materials with us to bus. But again as expected, Adam prohibited her from lifting even a pin (as she was wounded that should be precisely refered to as bruises) . But as a good girl and an obedient student she followed instructions of teacher~ offcourse not but of Adam for sure.

[6]

The same night, Navi posted pics of the picnic trip after reaching home. She didn't forget to mention Adam but here comes the twist. Adam didn't like even one picture of hers! She then sent a pic to sent a pic to Adam at private chat section. There Navi scolded Adam very mush , or to say too much. After that Adam apologized for the thing he hadn't done. Then he went and liked all her posts. After returning he said it's done. The. With slight sarcasm navi replied "As if you have done a favour to me!"

"May be!"

"Then thanks!

"Welcome!"

"Is it a formality?"

"Yes! But if yours gratitude was a formality."

[7]

Now this was all I could have told you about that trip. Now we should focus upon the matter from tutions. During this , we were easily able to see there efforts towards one another. Though they tried hard to hide all these nuisance but we knew them from days immemorable. Yet we weren't sure about there's so I personally kept a mum (and Avni too was silent about this matter these days)

[8]

In almost every treats at first tutions, this kind of moments were easily visible to give us proper hints. These included passing of food materials, sighting one another, helping over-capacitively of in same team , enjoying one another's non habitual madness,also noticing things that we were unaware of! Such as traces of cream over Navi's face or the dedication of Adam towards soft drinks. If we take in consideration the partying front ..... Wait! One more thing let me tell~ We were partying in second tutions and had momos. There were less pouches of sause than the crowd itself we somehow managed to get one pouch in between four persons ans Navi didn't get any. Then Adam did that was expected by anyone who is reader here. Now we must move out of partying front. When I and Avni were in our initial stages of relationship, let me clarify the that we wanted ours to work on grassroot level , it was time of something October And we wanted some time to have privacy and have some gossips with Avni . I am some shy short of person. Adam and Navi stood at some ten meters from us. The length of seperation between them showed a necessary bond is attraction and external egoistic repulsion. I focused upon Avni and they were busy in themselves. There were some instances when only four of us were in first tution. Then they used to walk whole park infinite times while we two sat to talk and that wasn't for there sake ~ according to them ~ this was for us. Quite good it seems..

[9]

This day should be referred to as a devastating bent in the situation of Adam and Navi, as it changed almost everything. We four and an additional boy were sitting at park to spend the time between two tutions. Then we started walking towards second tution. I alongwith Avni were walking several steps ahead of those three. Everything wasn't usual. This time there was an appreciable change in the position of Navi as she used to walk steps ahead of us and today she was beside Adam. Neither of us gave special attention to it . We had to take a turn which led our classes and the straight path wasn't of our concern. We were about to take turn but Navi from behind asked me not to turn and walk some distance ahead! I glanced at time which showed ten minutes to six, Means ten minutes extra! Okay!~I answered. We headed straight, but to our surprise he sent that extra guy towards tutions. Now basically the seen was that we two were a few steps and they were behind us maintaining the minimum distance so that our voices don't get mixed. Now I looked at Avni with a smile and she understood the sign language that I was noticing those two. But she gave a nudge to me and asked me in a slow voice to walk straight and not intrupt there discussion. After going some 100m we returned and Avni won the bet! They were in love! Finally they took me out of dilemma.

CHAPTER THREE

THE ACCEPTANCE

"Panic presents problem in a more macabre form to us."

~Joshit Mishra 'Uditanshu'

[1]

The same night as Adam and Navi had a peaceful walk, I got to realise that not everything was fine. When I had reached home I noticed about eighty unread whatsapp messages. But I had checked it well some ten minutes before! I supposed it to be some funny sort of matter in some groups.i changed my clothes and washed my face and then returned to my room And took mobile phone with the intention of freshening the mood for some fifteen minutes.

[2]

The counting had reached one and a half hundred. I opened and saw a group having some random name of its. I opened and basically the chatting there seemed to be second part of some discussion already done elsewhere. It mainly contained phrases like "It is a great trouble." "I might get restricted in home." "Mine future is too now destroyed." "Now nothing can be done!" " I'm feeling like crying." "There's no solution." " Maybe we are finished now!" " What will they think about us!" "Have we broken there trust?" " Why these problems for us?" " We haven't done a mere wrong deed!". I patiently read all those messages and now I doubted if everything was alright. As I reached the latest texts I saw there my name being repeated.. "Sid!" "Sid listen no!" "Here we are in big trouble..."~and some twenty texts of similar meaning in a line. Before replying them I checked the group members and there were three ~ Avni Navi and Me. Now I replied~

Sid:"yes I'm here speak flawlessly now."

Avni : "We are in a big trouble now Sid. I can't see any way out of it." I felt her at the edge of crying by the way she was feared . The first priority I gave to comfort them.

Sid: "Avni please calm down everything will be alright, don't worry, stay calm."

Avni : "No Sid! It isn't possible, our dreams are going to get spoiled, you ain't understanding it."

Navi: "You don't know about our parents. Our lives are going to be destructed."

Sid: "How can I try to understand when I don't even have a clue about it."

Navi: "Avni explain him. I'll be back soon after crying a bit".

Avni : "Sure! I'll too be back after crying a bit."

Sid: "Wait! Why the hell are you two getting this much worried?"

Navi: "You ain't understanding Sid!"

Avni : "Yes Sid!"

Sid: "First of all you two take deep breath."

Avni : "Okay!"

Sid: "Breath deeply and slowly. Now I think you got some stillness."

Avni : "Don't know!"

Sid: "Now tell me everything in as much detail as possible."

Avni : "Okay! As I was returning from Navi's home, a vagabond teenage of our colony 'B' stopped me."

Sid: "And I think he misbehaved and hence you think your parents will put restrictions on you."

Navi: "Listen to him first, you fool!"

Avni : "First Listen to me. It is far more complicated matter."

Sid: "Okay , I was just kidding! You proceed!"

Navi: "Here we are almost dying and you are kidding!"

Avni : "Sid get serious, it's much serious matter."

Sid: "Okay let Avni proceed!"

Avni : "Then B asked me to greet him , to avoid any conversation I said good evening and headed towards my home. Then again he blocked my way a few steps ahead and then he stated asking where do I go tutions. I replied that it was none of his buisness. He again said ' Success Classes' or just chilling with boys. I said 'what the rubbish you are talking about. I don't think you should poke your nose in any of ours matters'. He then said 'Shall I tell this to your brother and parents?' I ignored him and walked speedily towards my home . After reaching home I first of all texted Navi and till now neither of us has changed. We are in same clothing yet."

Navi: "Why these kind of people don't mind there own business."

Sid: "He won't do anything, otherwise he would have done so far."

Avni : "No Sid! You don't know him, he's ruined the lives of several girls of our colony in the similar way."

Sid: "First of all don't get panic otherwise problem is sure to get created at your home."

Navi: "We haven't spoken even a word to anyone and mom has surely noticed it. "

Avni : "Me too!"

Sid: "Oh lord! Don't get panic no! That would only add to our problems."

Avni : "What should we do now we don't have our minds at proper places."

Sid: "Okay okay first of all stay calm!"

Navi: "We can't."

Avni : "Have you informed Adam?"

Sid: "Why to make him worry?"

Avni : "Navi add him."

Sid: "I don't find any relevance here!"

Avni : "Wait a bit."

Sid: "Let me check him first then take any initiative"

Navi: "Okay!"

[3]

I checked for him. He replied. I informed them. They added Adam . Again they explained the whole matter to Adam. Adam first of all tried to comfort them but hardly 10 minutes was all ans he left the group and then neither replied nor hinted anything. Now Navi seemed hurted to me. I asked the reason and she didn't reply. I asked again. She said she liked him! I asked Avni If she could believe. She said that she knew it . Navi had told her earlier everything. Means I was the one who was most distrustful. Afterall Navi was something like heartbroken. Her one of the statement had hit me right at the heart. I remember it well word by word. Navi said to Avni " Tu bohot khuskismat hai , tera(bf) tere sath hai har halat me, mera to pehli mushkil me daga de gaya"{ You are very lucky to have your (boyfriend) in all the times you need him , and mine has dumped me in very first problem}. Above line has the capacity to well quote the pain of her. Then she had some conversations for almost an hour and the same pain was scattered all over her words. Lastly she agreed to wait and showed her acceptance towards behaviour of 'B' as well as Adam. Adam may not have dumped Navi but the abrupt exit , and ignorance made Navi think that she has been dumped. The way Navi was sad was a clear sign of her being too much emotionally attached with Adam. The belief of Navi that Adam must stand beside her in situation like this shows that they must had long discussions over this and they surely had expressed there feelings in a genuine way. I remained under my blanket with soo many thoughts. Well I didn't have any authentic clue so weaving soo many links I fell asleep.

CHAPTER FOUR

THE FAMILY TRIP

"*Family stands beside us no matter what the situation is.*

~Joshit Mishra Uditanshu"

[1]

That day took me about an hour to comfort those two and create within them a self confidence. They were now internally ready to face all that was about to come. But Navi...! I think this was a heart-wrenching moment for her. Next day she texted me on her own. And she chatted with me for some two hours straight! Yes I'm not kidding. Those were as follows→

"Sid!"

After a minute or so I replied- "Yes please!"

"I'm afraid now. Even more than yesterday. This one incident can fully spoil my dreams. If I had the authority the I must would have hung to death people like 'B' who interfere the privacy of others."

Let me clear a thing. Navi texted me at about 1 at noon and before her I had some conversations with Avni in chats. She seemed something strongly hurted only because I was fully supporting her and I was ready to solve the problems of her. Unbelievable no! Infact how can someone blindfolded believe another one only on the basis of his statements? She told me that navi was facing much more internal conflicts- one is due to B and another due to Adam as how can he leave her in such a situation! As it was visible from her conversation that I was supposed to do three works simultaneously

1. Solve the matter of B.
2. Know the ye truth of Adam.
3. Talk to Navi as she is in feeling broken up from first teenage love or probably crush or may be infatuation as she said it to be.

As Avni considered asam as her brother, ger words had sympathy towards him but sobbing of Navi had deep impact on her at the same time. Keeping all the above matters in my mind I replied-

"Be brave~. This isn't the Navi whome I texted some three months ago for the first time."

"Situation takes away all the ego.."

"That boy B isn't going to tell even a word to either of your parents. And if he tries to Blackman then we'll try to get a way out of it."

"That's not the main matter."

"Then?"

"Adam!"

"It means you surely had something fir him in your heart?"

"A very special corner. But it doesn't exists as I think!"

"I exists even now. He'll reoccupy it. You'll see!"

"I don't think so."

"But I think."

"No it can't."

"It must be. I know him for a long time. He is not this much cruel to break the heart of a cute girl."

"Thank you."

"Oh! You got to notice that word."

"I think so."

"Sounds good

"But he surely isn't that kind of bit who doesn't even speaks word in favour of mine."

"Do you mean that his sympathy would have sorted all problems?"

"Atleast majority of problems."

"I don't believe."

"After having conversations with you ,both Avni and me got a peaceful night with normal sleep."

"Oh!"

"But he is very much caring boy."

"He is."

"Then you should try today good?"

"19 times. I have sent him hii 19 times and reply of none."

"He may be himself in trouble."

"Buy not even a hint!"

"Wait for tomorrow. You should talk to him and clear this all."

"What should I talk? Everything is over now."

"How can you say that?"

"There is no possibility of that.."

"But you can focus upon positive aspects too , you can expect positive response from him."

"What should I do? I want to conserve it at any cost."

"Keep trying."

"Okay!"

"Noo! You should take your own time to solve this all I think."

"Okay;"

"I think I'll be there the next day with you. Okay that would be great."

"Fine!"

"Bye!"

"Bye!"

[2]

It was next day ~ The Monday. I woke up I noticed some unusual chaos and rush in my home. After sometime I got to realise that a family trip was today! But u was ought to be with Navi today at evening! I refused to go with them and they all gave me permission to stay at home. Wow! Now I could freemindedly help Navi. Buy at last moment when they were about to leave, my (jiju) brother in law asked me to join them ans I couldn't get any excuse that time and I too hot in the vehicle. At about 9 o' clock we left for destination. Meanwhile Navi and Avni were discussing the possibile outcomes of today's evening. Means this much tension on Saturday evening then a Sunday and then tutions at evening~ almost 40 hrs. How navi managed to handle these all, is out of my logics... What exactly the massages were us difficult to jot down here as there were about 2800 message conversation from 9 at morning to 4 at noon. But as we were heading towards temple of destination, I just quietly read messages and didn't reply any. Basically they had been discussing the negative aspects and the reasons for which Adam can break up. When we reached temple the. I turned off notifications ans put mobile in the pocket. We went in and performed worship. Lord Hanuman there seems just alive. Then we afe food and while we left for home , clock showed 3 PM. I opened whatsapp and started reading messages. It again just showed tension and negativity. Now I tried to make Navi believe that everything was going to be alright and Adam will never dump her. But she was just focusing on negative aspects of the situation. Somehow by 3:15 PM I managed to make her believe that everything was going to be alright. The. She left to get dressed up for tutions and Avni has done so 15 minutes earlier. Thus both reached outside tution by 3:42 PM. They texted. I just worked on Navi and tried to make her calm . Every minute passing not only raised out heartbeat but also created the peculiar mental situation that appears just 18 minutes before final results. Navi was nervous a lot. It was 3:48PM now. She started taking new tension now. She doubted if Adam would come this day. She got tensed for what would happen if he comes 15 minutes late. Adam in general is 15 minutes late at least. Well listening to the heartbeats, when it became 3:50PM , Adam arrived. He just stood some five minutes away from this duo. Navi was too nervous and even started trembling somewhat. She refused to face him. And at last Avni forced her to go and clear it all.. She got infront of Adam. Clock showed 3:52 PM.

Iasked"Has she approached?"

"She is walking towards him." ~ replied Avni

"Keep me updated with every moment."

"Okay! Adam is still standing like a log of wood ..... Navi has reached there..... She is saying something.... She is still speaking something..... Adam is standing quite. I can clearly notice a smile on his face..... Hope he confesses..... Why the heck is he not responding? ...Oh! Shit! Everything got ruined....God!"

"What happened?.... Avni speak no!.... What happened?"

"Q(girl from chapter one) has come."

"Oh shit!"

"Navi has come back near me."

"But why?"

"Don't know."

"She could have carried on conversation.."

"Send her back."

"She is refusing."

"Don't say that."

"Now she has gone again."

"Keep me updated."

"Q is now with me , they have got proper space of privacy."

"Good!"

"Why the heck is he not saying a mere word?"

"Why"

"He nodded. Navi is returning. I can't see a expression of happily. Break up!"

"What! Don't throw jokes at this moment."

"Seriously! It's a break up."

"Where is Navi?"

"In front of me."

"Support her"

"She mustn't cry. Though she has tears in her eyes, listen I'll talk to you later... Probably next day...Bye."

"Bye!"

The time now showed 3: 58PM. I kept mobile apart apart. After two hours we were at home I was too much tired ai went to bed at 7 o' clock. The time gap was used by me eating and having some YouTube time and other non-productive works.

[3]

It was the next day I met Navi ans talked to her about yesterday in that thirty minutes gap between tutions. The.

She told me the sequence of events after I left. Avni was with ud and Adam was at stadium playing cricket. Basically what she told is ahead→

"Yesterday was the saddest day I've ever lived. But I never expected that. He never seemed this much cruel."

"I agree."

"He was so considerate and caring for me. But yesterday he showed his reality. "

"How did you managed to be normal yesterday?"

"Actually I felt like crying in first tution itself. Somehow I managed to stop myself from crying. Then we went directly to the second tution and sat there for almost half an hour. I didn't talk to anyone. Then I went home . My father had an album in his hands. He was staring at my childhood pictures. Because of memories he was too emotional. I went near him. Slept beside him. My head was on his shoulders. I couldn't resist mu tears there. We become the real us in front of father. Seeing my tears and the emotions from pictures in album, Dad's eyes got filled with tears. Now I cried heavily. My mom then got in and sympathized me. Everyone thought that it was due to adorable memories that I got in through pictures. But internal me knew the real matter. After that I wept out my tears and went to my room. There I sat on bed for almost two hours doing nothing. Just tears and memories of Adam. I was feeling bad but at the same time was expecting him to return back into my life. After two hours my mom came in my room and made me eat dinner. She at last asked if something went seriously wrong. I said that it was like break up of freindship. She just patted on my head say there for almost ten minutes in order to prevent me from crying and seeing that in front of her I cried even more she just somehow managed to calm me down and then she went out and my granny came to sleep. Then I didn't wanted to show my tears to her that must had created a tension for her too. I turned my face towards wall and pulled blanket over face. I can easily remember that I hardly slept that night. In place of ambitious dreams, Adam's moment came to my mind and end of every part was just terrible.I just kept gazing at the corner of my room.Now I feel sleepy. But why should I sleep when I don't have Adam to dream of. Listen I need solitude now. Bye!"

"Bye"

She didn't even saw my bye text....

CHAPTER FIVE

NAVI'S PERSPECTIVE

[1]

Following few days , I was in contact with navi. She was something like heartbroken. But I wasn't ready to accept that a strong hearted girl like her was easily shattered into pieces in just 4 days relationship?? I mean whenever I talked to her , she seemed me a very ambitious and focused girl. She took decisions at once that too were good enough to stick with. But nowadays the confidence and a sense of stiffness was gone from her words. Indeed she felt on herself that some greater aspect of her life was gone. I felt sorry for her but didn't expressed it because whenever she had asked for advice , I always favoured Adam.

Lets Start from first week. During this time she wasn't ready to accept the fact that Adam has left her that was a sort of break up. During this , I was expecting a patch up but again I was wrong. They behaved like likely charged bodies and repelled one another. They didn't even speak a word . Once or twice I noticed them staring at another secretly but that wasn't any hint this time (though it was a hint for me not more than a fortnight before) . She now started saying that it was nothing now. No corner for Adam in her heart. She now seemed again totally stable and after a week she seemed normal . It was a good sign that it didn't affected her drastically. Though it did but not as other's who on being broken heart , attempted suicide by drinking a glass full phenyl (that doesn't even kills germs on flore,Lol!).

[2]

Now all things became fine. After our 11th class examination it came a period when we were waiting for our results. During This time I casually messaged navi and she was something like ill since last few days but that day she was just alright. We started our conversations. Avni had told me a day earlier that navi still sometimes goes deep into Adam's dreams. She sometimes seems lost in imagination. Now I thought it might work if I force her to spill out everything about Adam in front of me to rise up of all this. Now the rest of conversation is ahead→

"So you do think he has done something destruction in my life."

"Yes exactly this is what I think."

"But you are absolutely wrong this time mr. Sid. I am properly normal as I see."

"But you ain't no!" "So what makes you think so?"

"Your behaviour these times."

"So what's odd in my behavior?"

"You don't even speak a word with Adam."

"So what, I didn't even speak a month earlier"

"But this is a drastic change I see"

"So you might have noticed the wrong aspects of things.."

"And your smile and quarrelsomeness that is gone too, what do you have to defend that?''

"This must be a good sign for you as this might bring a stillness."

"But you ain't normal for sure."

"See Sid, I've totally forgotten whatever has happened recently."

"I don't think this a matter having only recent roots."

"Yes it is truth."

"You two were liking one another from a quite long time."

"Oo hello! That might be truth but he is the boy who poked his nose for only 4 days."

"So basically it is a 4 day relationship that you are referring to"

"Much similar''

"And you two have had break up"

"There wasn't any thing that should be referred to as break up. We were something more than friends and that proved out to be just infatuation. So I don't think there are break up of infatuation.."

"But I wanted to say that 6 days ain't enough to get this much attached. This all has somewhat a long chain of events." ''Listen Sid I've totally forgotten that all.. and I expect the same from you too."

"Shall a talk to Adam over this Matter once? That won't do anything."

"Oh ! I was absent for one day and you have created this much fuss.."

"Oh ! You do think I'm the victim"

"When I sounded like that?"

"I think you do"

"Listen! We should talk about it sometime else."

"I think so ."

"Bye"

"Ba bye."

[3]

It was the day of results. We all had performed well and result was far better than our expectations. That day I had somewhat longer conversations with Navi and then I got to know that I was wrong one more time. I thought that everything has got correct but this was not true. Basically after having long discussion over results and asking the results of even those people whome I never said even a word , I asked about Adam's result as though I knew it. She asked me to never again talk about him. Now this created an unsuppressable curiosity. Not more than a week before she said that he meant nothing for her and now she is refusing to even listen his name! This much aggressive behaviour is a sign of internal weakness~ I had read it in one of those personality development or success tips books. I tried to calm her out and she became calm. But at the same time she became emotional and spitted all the matter. →

"I never expected that."

"Me too!"

"He wasn't that kind of guy."

"Hmm.."

"What hmm , you always kept taking his sides."

"After all he's my best friend."

"Better say was.."

"Nope!'

"Means you still have a sympathy towards him."

"There's nothing like sympathy I see"

"Whatever!"

"Atleast for me."

"During starting days he used to talk as if honey is dropping from his mouth. And eventually he ended like this.."

"Do you still have some corner for him?"

"I really loved him.. I still expect that he'll come back and say that it was all a prank.. many a times I'm lost in his thoughts. During nights sometimes I cry , I don't know why? , but his thoughts make me cry, we'd dreamt many things, shattered into pieces now."

"Means your anger towards him is only external.''

"What had I done ? What was my mistake? Means he didn't even speak a word that day. He stood like a portrait and had a dreadful smiled. Those 6 days were the first time when I started believing that not all boys are non-trustworthy . But he shattered that too."

"But you are now sharing these things with me."

"Listen, one who stands with us during our bad times becomes a reliable person. So you must be a exception among all those unreliable boys."

"But it's only four weeks since we became friends!"

"That shouldn't matter I see."

"Hope so. "

"He was soo much caring dude. He isn't the same Adam with whome I fell in ..."

"Maybe he's in some problem..."

"Sid please.. don't take his side atleast now."

"Okay."

"But he could have talked to me no!"

"Yes he should have."

"But he hasn't yet."

"Sorry,! But I must leave now"

"Why?"

"To celebrate my results."

"All boys are same!"

"No no I didn't meant that(said I laughingly)."

"I'm kidding, congratulations again to shatter records."

"Thanks!"

[4]

Time passed by and it was almost 1 month since that all . I rarely noticed what navi was facing and only focused upon syllabus for 12th. But again lockdown and our regular classes got stopped and again I started studying by self. But within 15 days I realised that I must spend some of my time doing some refreshing activities as this would enhance my capacities. During same time I coincidentally texted navi in place of Avni and then the way she talked was something superb.

"Hey!"

"Hello!"

"What's up?"

"Atleast you don't ask these rubbish.."

"Ok!"

"So what about your studies?"

"On track. Atleast better than school!"

"Hahaha!"

"And yours?"

"I fell ill so it's a break."

"Have you recovered now?'

"Yes!"

"The way you sound , I think you have no worries."

"Exactly! And I don't think you should believe that that Adam can still affect my life or dreams."

"I think you have got offended ..."

"No no , there's nothing like that."

"So can I know what the exactly happened between you two?"

"Ah! As I don't care a bit about this so we can discuss it ..."

"So when did you two started conversation?"

"Basically during 9th I just knew that there is some Adam in our class but in next section. Then it was after tenth that he followed me in insta and I followed back ...."

"Wait wait wait..."

"What now?"

"I just wanted to know how you two fell in relationship and as far as I know you were together for hardly a week."

"Oh! It means mr. Sid believes that one can fall in love in just 1 sec.."

"Atleast this was mine case"

"But mine was purely normal case,it's not unique like yours and always remember yours is still working and mine has been demolished."

"Ok sorry for the intruption"

"Don't try to satire"

"Okay no!"

"Now listen! I followed him back then whenever I uploaded a story he used to replying it. Basically it was proceeding in the same manner unless we bacame frank in tution. Then we became friendly and as you know there were quarrels between us infact every day ."

"Yes we noticed that all.."

"Yeah! So we were nearly as like friends. We used to hit one another and all the things were going on the track. Then it was somewhat like starting of December and he asked for some notebook I remember. He needed it so that he may copy it and make it completed. The next day I forgot. And he became hyper. It was in a way that I never noticed before. You clearly know my nature that I don't tolerate even a word spoken against me , but I was like a dumb before him . He continued scolding me and I stood like a portrait. Then I left the spot without saying a word and for even my surprise I took my notebook on my own and handed over to him and even said sorry! Quite amazing. Means I am a girl who don't apologise when it's my mistake and I apologized because he became hyper. My mind had surely got crashed. But at that time what I felt for him is infact inexpressible in words. Then this all continued and I got more and more interested over him . Means every step of him was a anesthesia for me! I felt myself consciously unconscious over his dreams. You shouldn't make an image if only I'm the one who is interested. Infact he was too. Do you remember those times when you and Avni used to sit together to have some nice talks and at the same time we used to roam around the park . Those were a gift for me that I'd got on your behalf and even you didn't knew. Walking beside him and noticing each and every thing was like .... Was like everything. Once at that moments he made a swing vacant for me. He was so caring you know. Do you remember that time when we four played red hands and you were sitting at a distance. And then when Avni 's hands were paining you came closer to her , took her hand in you hand and tried to comfort her. I noticed that being a great moment for you two as you never sat this much closer before. You were busy in yourself and at the same time my hand was in hand of Adam. He too was trying to decrease the pain in same manner as you were trying for Avni ."

"Wow! Means a random guy comforts you."

"No he wasn't a random guy. Infact we both knew that we are having mutual crush but neither showed the courage."

"Ok! Proceed!"

"Hm.. Then you remember our picnic trip. It was basically mid December. So there I hit him many times but he didn't spoke even a word. When I wounded myself in my leg then he ran here and there and managed that turmeric powder. After that he didn't let me do even a single work. He filled up water bottles for me . He was with me when we sat for eating and even when we washed our dishes. When we were returning he prohibited me from carring any load. When I reached home then I tagged him in story of the picnic trip and then he didn't even showed any interest over it . Means he should have liked my posts and should have commented. I Stubbornnessly messaged him and forced him to like all those posts. At the same time he went and followed whatever I said. It was only Iniciative at insta,the main events were at whatsapp. Then After liking all posts he asked for some pics of spot and hence we shifted to whatsapp. So after that notebook incident he texted me for the first time and after this pics incidence we had something like an hour of conversation. We then talked about all the fun we had , all the pretty clashes that we had. He seemed somewhat inclined towards me. The next day I noticed him more polarized towards me, those clashes continued but ended with some more closeness.. I sent every thing to Avni and she was cent percent sure that Adam was having a strong and unsuppressable crush on me."

"Wait! Means Avni knows everything?"

"Yes!"

"But she hasn't even speak a word before me!"

"I asked her to keep it secret."

"Means she has the capability to keep secrets and digest it"

"Hahaha Yes!"

"Proceed.."

" For two days our routine was same. We had conversation before tutions and then tutions where he came earlier because I asked him to come so that we may had gossips before classes started. We had more pretty fights and then at second day's end we were having text conversations after tutions and it was something like 9 o clock. Adam asked me something and I said something to him which made him angry and then we didn't talked any more. Then next day no conversation before tutions. Then at tutions I didn't even notice him. Then before second tutions he asked a girl to bring chocolate for him and she bought for him and then they together ate chocolates to make me Jealous. That day I had posted a status at whatsapp and in order to reply it Adam texted me after tutions . As I was somewhat interested in this so I quickly replied. He asked about my mood and then those nonsense pretty texts. After having conversation for some ten or twenty minutes he asked me if I liked him . So I was just confused what to reply. Means I was pretty sure that I have strong feel of attachment and the only correct answer was absolutely Yes. I agreed. Then I asked the same question from him .He asked what I expected as his answer. Absolutely I expected a firm concent from his side. I told him this .He too agreed. At that moment my happiness was at it's peak. I means felt myself being the most lucky girl. I don't think you need to be explained the feeling that you get when your crush has a crush back on you. Means the best feeling. Then he started his foolishness and asked "what do you mean by liking me?" Then it took me ½ hours to satisfy him with what I meant by like .."

"Atleast that is only half hour, Avni explained me for almost ......"

"Listen to me first"

"Ok then speak"

"Then that night was the most queer night . I mean I was happy or to say something greater than happiest. I wanted to sleep so that I could meet him in my dreams and talk with him in any way that I wanted but ... I was dreaming with my eyes open , I couldn't sleep , my grandmother was sleeping beside me and I was lying on bed facing towards wall so that she can't notice. Oh! How I spent that night was the matter of excitement. When my eyes got closed I don't remember...."

"Okay boss that night must have been great but shall we move next."

"Sun to re...(listen to me first..)"

"Okay okay!"

"You are too impatient bro!"

"You proceed..."

"Then the next day. I was at home and almost every family member asked me why I was soo much happy. I just said it's nothing special, but you know how special was it for me. I did everything that I was expected to do and before 10 o' clock I took my android. Actually I was waiting for him to message..I just watched many vedios and spent my time here and there just scrolling the screen. Finally it was 12 noon and guess what...?"

"Adam texted you..?."

"You are absolutely wrong . My grannie came and I was called up for Lunch. Then again my happiness was noticed by everyone, I was trying to hide my smile but I couldn't..I quickly finished my meal and rushed towards my bed. It was the same place where I am used to using mobile. Now clock showed 1 o' clock. Now I thought he must have forgotten that he's got a cute and innocent girlfriend last evening..."

"Wait wait wait... Do you want to say that he proposed someone else last night and you were expecting messages for you"

"O hello! I'm that cute and innocent girl"

"Ooo ok ok proceed"

"Means there exist some people who can't tolerate someone else's positive appraisal. Okay let's move to our context. I finally texted him at about 1:30PM and for my surprise I got to know that he's been waiting for me since morning. What a rubbish coincidence. He said that he didn't texted me because of the fear if someone of my family see them then it would have been a problem for me. Then we had many sweet talks and then when we were in tutions I noticed him blushing and I was too blushing Wait! That day he was something like appreciating me. He said that I had soft cheeks. He always hit me on cheeks and the reason for this was that I had soft cheeks. When I told Avni this. She said that even Sid won't have any idea about Avni 's cheeks and here Adam has got to know . For next two days this all went the same way. Those thirty minutes walks were a gift for me. He used to help me everywhere and his caring had it's own peaks. We used to have nice conversations during afternoon and then sighting at tutions then walking side by side having long Discussions. Most important thing, what we discussed didn't matter, we just kept stretching the conversation longer and longer. Meanwhile a test in both the tutions. For the first time I crossed 25/30 at first tution and this gave me an impression that studying free minded can surely give better results. All was quite right and cheerful for four days. We were in so called healthy relationship. Then it was the most unpredictable day. As we reached turning, Adam for my surprise asked you to walk some more distance ahead and sent away the boy walking with us . That day we'd some nice talks then that random boy intruption and his Stupidness led to our break up as you know. Then as you know I was totally broken up. That day as you know God created some favourable circumstances for me and I cried over my dad's shoulder. Then to totally overcome that 4 day relationship it took complete six months."

"What about Adam?"

"Don't have clear idea."

"Ok!"

"Listen! Don't tell this to anyone"

"Buy I've shared this to one of my friend (that is author)"

"Tell me that you haven't disclosed our identity."

"I've!" "How can you be such a dumb and fool!"

"Sorry!"

"Please ask that boy to keep identity a secret."

"Wait (after some time) he's agreed. He won't disclose anything but he's planning a Book."

"Fine! He may write it but ask him to be careful in order to avoid any problems for me."

"Ok!(after sometime) he is requesting you to write foreword for his book."

"Let's see what can I do for it."

[5]

One week passed by and I told you all this . Now I again texted navi to get to know what the Adam was facing. After having some casual chattings I came straight to the point. This time it was really hard to confess her.

"I'm not going to speak even a word over this matter now"

"Please !"

"I've forgotten all that rubbish. Last time I told you so that you can get clarify and never ever raise this topic in front of me."

"Please.. listen I'm your brother! And you can do atleast this for me."

''I don't want to re-memorise that cheater again."

"Have you two talked about this again? Haven't you?"

"No .. because all he said was a lie. He's a lier"

''You should have talked to him atleast once."

"No! I don't want to discuss upon the matter of that cheater again. "

"Please please please !"

"Ok but only in one condition.."

"Which condition?"

"You will never raise this matter again."

"Okay I'm ready!"

"Ask whatever you want to know clearly.'

"What were the conversions between you?"

"Oh he always kept asking questions."

"It's my charecteristics ."

"Yeah!"

"Which type of questions?"

"As like why I like him."

"And what is the answer?"

"It's irrelevant now."

"Means what lies you kept in answer then.."

"He was very caring one, I didn't find anything like a sign of cheater but still he cheated on me."

"There must be some incident which made you trust him."

"Once I visited one of My friend's house and asked him not to message and he didn't. When I asked why then his reply was the flirtiest one. But still he was just cheater"

"What cheater? Tell me just one lie of him."~ I texted with the spirit of friend of Adam "When I asked him about his first crush..."

"That is a far irrelevant matter. He had that crush when he was in just class seventh or so."

"Listen to me first.. he said just forget about her . He said that she didn't matter for him any more but the reality was that he never exerted her out of his heart. Damn lier . I hate him...."

"Are you two still friends?"

"No ."

"Means no conversion?"

"We talk face to face normally but no texting."

"What about his behaviour?"

"It kept changing frequently after break up. Means he still likes you but don't want to express it because he's got in some trouble or ego.."

"But why?"

"I don't know. Can you memorise any incident in which he showed caring attitude towards you after break up?"

"During playing red hands, a boy hit me hard , then he holded my hand firmly as it was paining a lot."

"Have you discussed this matter again?"

"No!"

"Can you tell me what were the discussions that day when I was absent and you talked to him outside tution?"

"I approached him. He was smiling. I asked what happened. He replied nothing. I asked if I should consider it all over. It was very hard to listen a yes from him."

"Don't you have the way to confess something?"

"I don't think starting in positive way could have helped me.."

"What exactly were you discussing that day that required an extra time and you asked us to walk straight??"

"How could we had talked in front of that boy?"

"During free time he went stadium. Means we got enough time but weren't satisfied. So he somehow managed to send him away and asked me to confess you to walk straight. "

"What conversations did you two have that day?"

"Random talks .."

"Like?"

"Like I said it's pretty cold and he replied sorry I can't take off jacket for you as if I expected his jacket. Then he asked if you knew about us. Then I replied that only Avni knew. When we're alone then only I was the one to speak and he just smiled and answered my questions."

"Ooo!"

"Somewhere in those 4 days of relationships I texted him in midnight just to show him the sixteenth pages of physics that I wrote. He replied me instantly and he was writing English. He urged me to take rest and I said that I had taken promise to complete it. He asked in whose name , and I said in his then he said me to write as long as I wanted but at the same time asked me to necessarily take rest. He was very much caring."

"As if sixteenth pages are some mountain peaks..!'

' "Why not! I wrote just to show him otherwise I never sacrificed my sleep for studies."

"Ohooo Adam haa ...!"

"Listen this is all that I could tell you and now I'm feeling extremely sleepy so I'm going to have nice sleeps."

"Ok!"

"Just pray that he doesn't come to my dreams"

''By god's grace"

"Bye"

"Bye"

As per promise I didn't texted her about this matter again. His dp in subsequent days was a bird flying away from a cage. This was symbolic representation of moving on. Atleast this was a better stage.

CHAPTER SIX

ADAM'S PERSPECTIVE

[1]

After having discussion with navi over Adam's matter for the last time , I talked to Avni over this matter-

. "So you want to know about those Navi and Adam."

"No!"

"You have just asked!"

"First of all tell me why you haven't disclosed it earlier?"

"Because Navi asked to keep it as secret."

"So what?"

"I have told you everything about me but won't tell about secrets of anyone."

"Ok!"

"Now ask me whatever you were looking for!"

"Do you know exactly why Adam abruptly ended his relationship with navi?"

"I have had only one conversation with Adam over this matter and whatever he told me was enough for me to get him innocent tag."

"And what he told ?"

"That day his father saw him texting navi. Then next day navi texted him about seventeen times and he ignored it all. Now you tell me what should he had done then?" "He should follow whatever his father had said him to do"

"Exactly!"

"But what about Navi?"

"Now at this point I'm too confused. There is no mistake of Navi but she has suffered this all. Adam is innocent because there is nothing in his hands. Now one is victim but none is culprit! It's queer situation. So I decided to stand with Navi as she needed emotional support."

"Ok!"

"But as I felt talking to Adam he too was something like suffering from same situation as Navi."

"Now I don't have any point on how to make my stand now."

"No need to make stand!"

"But now I think I'm the wrong doer here!"

"Listen! Whatever you have done is sitting apart and observing whatever happened. When you were asked for help then you did what seemed like the justice. So don't feel like wrong."

"But..."

"Can you consider India as one who is responsible for destruction of palestine ?"

"No!"

"You are india in this case."

"Hope so."

"And Sid! Listen! One more thing. What I personally think is that we should take a break from this all."

"(A stillness)"

"I think we should take our routes and do for our aims. "

"(A poise stillness)"

"And I thought like discussing this with you."

"Can I know the reason?"

"Well those two are well focused now and even more focused in studies then ever so I thought like this. If you don't find any point in this so we may continue this all..."

"No!No! I've got your point. So what is the best thing to say now is 'take care, ba bye '" "Bye!"

Her Persuasion skills are superb as you see. The comparison she made was fabulous. In Navi's case there is no culprit and all sufferers. I don't feel like discussing mine here. Hope this yields better results.

[2]

Before taking this all to conclusions and making a one sided opinion, I talked to Adam about this all. This gave more clear picture of whatever happened.

"So you may ask whatever you want"

" tell me all about the Navi's case."

"This may take a longer time."

"I can wait!"

"Okay!"

" start!"

"From where?"

"From point zero."

"Okay she came to our school in class ninth or eight or seventh . It must be eighth or ninth. I don't remember it well."

"Is it this much long.. means you are about to pic story from first day."

"Hmm!"

"Proceed..!"

"Then first day."

"Hmm..!"

"Second day...... Third day..... Fourth day... Fifth day....."

"Okay I know everything till 365th day now proceed."

"366th day..."

"Be serious no!"

"Ok!"

"Speak now!"

"Okay. While we stood with you all then we talked casually in 11th tutions. Then I asked for pics of picnic and she gave me in whatsapp. Then we had some conversations that I really don't remember now. It continued for next two days and then she proposed me. It was probably 9 in the evening and then I just seen that message and didn't replied. Then next day she didn't talked to me . That day I had eaten chocolate without asking her and then I texted her at evening as her mood was off whole day. Listen Sid I want to clear a thing. I wasn't a bit intrested in this all and has made clear earlier when you asked me outside stadium. That night I didn't answered in order to not hurt her. Next evening I texted her and asked how her mood was and then I asked some questions to know how much she was interested. I asked what her behaviour would have been if he said no or what would it have been if he said yes. Her answers were somewhat very emotional. She said "if it is yes then I will be extremely happy. And if it was no then I'll be be broken from inside" . Then I asked what she expected from me. She said yes! And I said consider whatever you want. Then she said yes and went back. Then next day I asked for extra walk and sent that extra guy back and asked you to not take turn. That was in order to confess her. I wanted to deny her in such a manner that she doesn't get hurted. But that day I wasn't able to muster up the courage to say anything. Then that boy intrupted and met Avni and threatened her whatever. That day I wanted to be with you trio and sort out problem but my dad asked for mobile as he needed to use whatsapp. I immediately left the group and then gave mobile to dad. Then I started thinking about it and found that whatever I wanted to do has been done without I even had a bit of work done. The next day Navi approached me and asked if everything was over. I wanted to support her at that time as she was emotionally unstable at that time. Tears were visible at that time in her eyes as if ready to roll down. But I made my heart strong and just said hmm that indicated that everything has got ended up."

CHAPTER SEVEN

EPILOGUE

I told Navi whatever Adam told me. She said that now she felt that her decisions were right though she was wrong. She said she had loved the right person and don't have any regrets for it. While Saying this sentence, tears rolled by her cheeks. She then said further "I did never expect love from her side. What I expected was care. And he cared as much as he could have. I had been considering him as culprit. I till today considered him as a cheap guy, a cheater and what not!. Now I feel anger on myself. I was the one who was wrong."

"No!"

"Don't try to comfort me this time. Let me cry! Can we talk sometime else?"

"Sure but don't cry no! Theirs is nothing like your mistake."

"I know there was mistake of no one. Whatever happened was absolutely right.

This will be last time I'll cry over this Matter. He's such a nice guy and I had surely made better choice. I'll never fall in love with anyone again. But I'll always remember this."

"Please don't cry.....!"

She left. Now I'll never raise this matter and never discuss this matter.

Adam is right in his place because he never intended to hurt Navi. He always kept seeking a safe way to deny. Navi surely had a strong attachment with Adam but she now will never get herself emotionally unstable due to this. Avni always noticed whatever was visible from the actions from Navi. She kept herself with Navi when she needed her best. I'm too a emotional kind of guy as Navi and Avni is emotionally though as Adam. So she took a diversion along with never creating problem for me . I just kept following whatever destiny gave me..

Destiny that put so many troubles for Navi as said by herself...... Well the story of Avni is far much intersting than this . I'll tell that later. Seeing this all I wrote a poetry. Lastly let's put it here→

Destiny

[1]

Destiny;
the ruiny.
It's nothing,
More than everything.
It is like waves,
Moving within dark caves.
One moment it is beside,
Another–opponent's side.
It is an unread book,
Which kept our minds shook.
It is already by almighty written,
Kept in some lion's den.
Never–the looser can pridict,
But for it conquerers are addict.
They are used to having future,
And then nurture.
There aims – many,
With destiny.

[2]

For us it contains almost nothing,
But we do believe that something.

There exists apart from womb and graves,
That creates within us braves.
To give them a tougher fight,
Force destiny to do with us right.
To ask to have over us a look,
That beside pawn we atleast are rook.
Many a times we are badly beaten,
But we are those who from lions den.
Has capability to fulfil desire,
And make the world admire.
To show them that they may be,
Gifted by god's politemost mercy.
But we aren't god gifted,
Neither our destiny is predicted.
It is our hands to write all,
Everything–aim to which our soul call.
Then have the hardest work ever,
And fight from the almighty giver.
Again the same procedure is repeated,
And alas! Again we are defeated.
Wins the tyranny,
Because of destiny.

[3]

The main story begins now,
We dare to see results somehow.
Then the unbelievable – quite new,
Feelings are generated – but a few.
Those forces to have cowardice acts,
And supports itself by illogical facts.
That are one – sided coin,
With no positive side got define.

The acts range from give up,
To finish repenting for the top.
That we are the unluckiest,
But we forget that the best.
Within us is yet to come,
That needs firstly to overcome.
From this hovoc and the best effort,
Use that only percent luck you got.
Within adverse conditions try,
Well we have another path to cry.
Over bad luck n' only a percent luck,
But we've to put on this path a jerk.
We'll use that weapons and,
Dominate over the fertilemost sand.
We'll become queen and even king,
We'll knockout n' rule over the ring.
The arena will be ours,
That we've to snatch from others.
And mine will be every penny,
After overcoming destiny.

Joshit Mishra 'Uditanshu'

9 798887 729374

Printed by Libri Plureos GmbH in Hamburg, Germany